Bella's Fall Coat

BY **Lynn Plourde**

ILLUSTRATED BY **Susan Gal**

Disnep · HYPERION

LOS ANGELES   NEW YORK

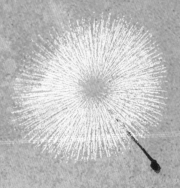

For information address Disney • Hyperion, 125 West End Avenue, New York, New York 10023.

First Edition, September 2016

Printed in Malaysia

10 9 8 7 6 5 4 3 2 1
FAC-029191-16166
Library of Congress Cataloging-in-Publication Data
Plourde, Lynn.
Bella's fall coat / by Lynn Plourde ; illustrated by Susan Gal.—First edition.
pages cm
Summary: "A picture book about the fall season, centering on Bella, a little girl who has outgrown but does not want to give up her favorite coat made by her grandmother, and how she deals with the inevitable change to something new"—Provided by publisher.
ISBN 978-1-4847-2697-6
(1. Autumn—Fiction. 2. Coats—Fiction. 3. Grandmothers—Fiction. 4. Change—Fiction.)
I. Gal, Susan, illustrator. II. Title.
PZ7.P724Be 2016
(E)—dc23   2014049052

Reinforced binding

Visit www.DisneyBooks.com

With love to Beckett, who makes Memsy's heart overflow
—LP

For Aunt Marie Debreczeni, with love and cherished memories
—SG

Bella was little.
But not as little as she used to be.

Grams tsk-tsked. "You're going to burst your buttons, girl. It's time for a new coat."

Bella shook her head. "No, Grams. This coat is my *favorite*. You made it for me, and I want to wear it *forever*!"

"Bella Marie, nothing lasts forever. Winter will be here soon—"

But **WHOOSH!**
Bella was already outside.

Bella twirled and whirled.

She crinkled and crackled.

She dove down deep
and pop-popped back up.

When Grams jangled the lunch bell, Bella burst into the kitchen.

"Eek!" Grams screamed. "A leaf monster!"

Bella giggled. "It's just me, Grams. Fall leaves are my *favorite*. Let's keep them *forever!*"

"Well, I know a way we can keep them for a little while," said Grams.

After lunch, Grams said, "Now, Bella, about that coat—"

But **WHIZZ!**

Bella was already outside.

She picked and plucked.

She stretched and reached.

She crunched
and munched.

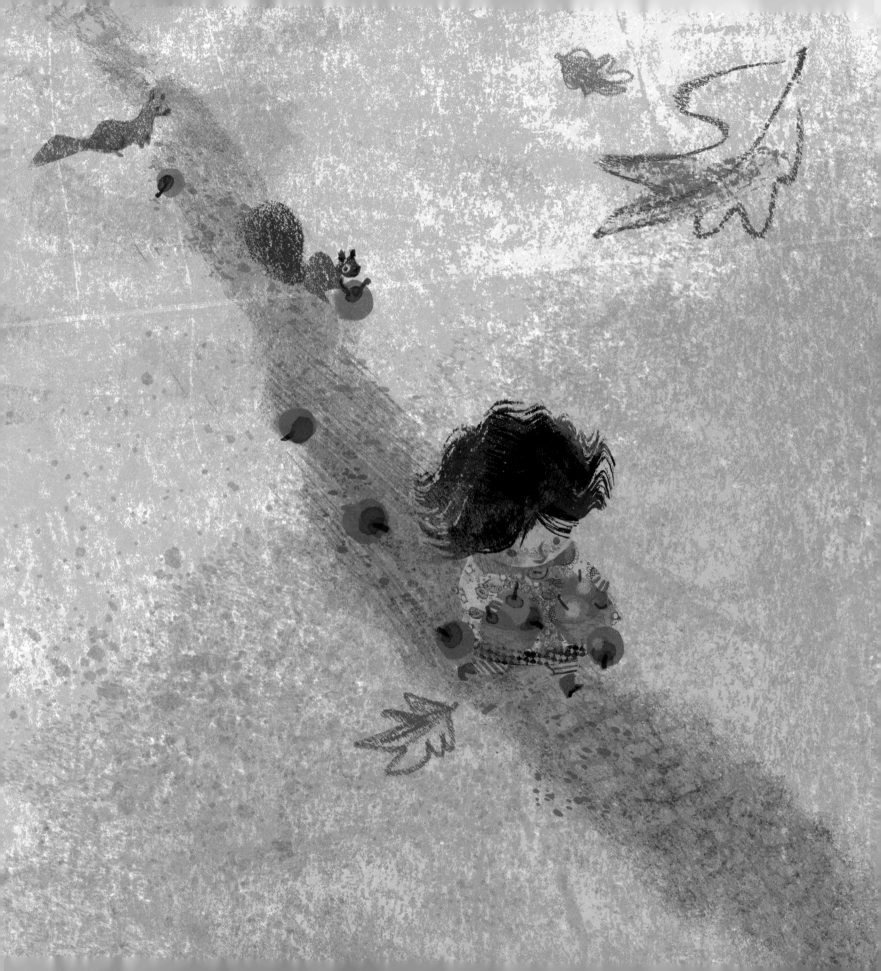

"Grams, my coat has pockets big enough for a whole tree of apples!" said Bella. "Can we make an apple pie? My *favorite*!"

"Hmm," said Grams.
"I'm sure we can make something with these."

After supper (with warm
apple tarts for dessert),
Grams tried once more.
"Your coat, Bella. It—"

But *ZOOM!*
Bella was already outside.

She sneaked and snooped.

She honked
and whistled.

She flapped and flew.

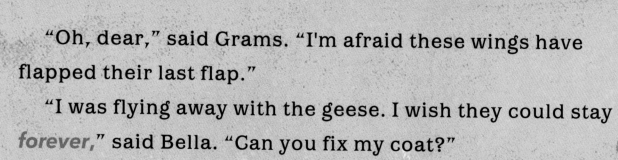

"Oh, dear," said Grams. "I'm afraid these wings have
flapped their last flap."

"I was flying away with the geese. I wish they could stay
forever," said Bella. "Can you fix my coat?"

"Let's see what I can do," said Grams.
"But now it's time for you to get ready for bed."

Grams tucked Bella in tight. The little girl
who wasn't quite so little fell asleep and
dreamed of her favorites—

bright orange leaves,

crisp, juicy apples,

and soft, white feathers.

Meanwhile . . .
Grams snipped and clipped.

She pushed and pulled.

She whirred and . . .

snored.

The next morning, Bella awoke—her eyes filled with white flakes.

"The first snow!" said Bella. "Can I go out and play in it?"

"Not in your old coat, you can't," said Grams.

"You couldn't fix it?" Bella said, her eyes filling with tears.

"No, kitten. I'm afraid you're going to have to wear this one instead."

Bella slipped it on.

She twirled and whirled.

She stretched and flapped.

She even found surprises in the
deep, deep pockets.

"Grams, this is my new *favorite* coat. Thank you! I will wear it *forever*!"

Bella saw her old coat drooping on a chair, sad and lonely.

She picked it up.

Grams asked, "Where are you going with—"

But SWOOSH!

Bella was already outside.

"That coat fits her perfectly,"
said Grams.

"Of course!" said Bella. "It's her **favorite!**"